Copyright © 2024 Nabiwabook
All rights reserved.
By Kwon Park
Translation by K. H. Yoo
Designed by Joe Fitz

Tel: 010-8227-8359
Website: nabiwabook.com
E-mail: nabiwabook2021@naver.com
Instagram: instagram.com/nabiwabook_publisher
Blog: blog.naver.com/nabiwabook2021

ISBN: 979-11-989928-0-2
Publication Registration: 2024.12.20

This is a work of fiction. The names, characters, places, and incidents portrayed in it are either are the product of the author's imagination or are used fictitiously. Any resemblance to actual persons, living or dead, events or locales, is entirely coincidental.

All rights are reserved. No part of this publication may be reproduced, stored in a retrieval system, or transmitted in any form or by any means, electronic, mechanical, photocopying, recording or otherwise, without prior permission of the publishers.

THE GOVERNOR'S CASE FILE

Kwon Park

Translated by K. H. Yoo

나비와북
Nabiwabook

THE GOVERNOR'S CASE FILE

* 이방/*Lee Bang: An occupation and title; an administrator who serves as the local assistant to the governor*

My precious village. Though it is a small town, nestled in the mountains, it has come a long way since its founding. The few citizens we have are simple and pure, causing no headaches for me. It seems like just yesterday, that cold winter day I was appointed to this post. Yet it is already spring—look how the village is awash in green! The mere sight of the large mountains peeking over the fence fills my heart with pride. That day, too, I was enjoying the simple pleasures of my office, looking out the window as I exhaled a contented sigh. Lee Bang, who was usually always near, was nowhere to be seen. Late afternoon approached, and the village was quiet and still. A wonderfully peaceful day. "I shall have a cup of tea," I said to myself. "It will go well with the confections brought to me by my nephew just a few days prior."

"Honored Governor! Sir!"

I had spoken too soon. Upon hearing the panicked voice and hurried footsteps approaching from afar, I picked up my hat and hurriedly placed it back on my head. Usually a calm man, Lee Bang looked far from tranquil as he came nearer and nearer. Kicking up a flurry of dust, Lee Bang ran through the courtyard and looked up at me, hesitating.

"Is something the matter?"

"Well sir, the matter is..."

Where was the man who had sprinted so urgently toward me? Lee Bang hemmed and hawed, opening his mouth then closing it again. I watched him silently for several seconds.

"Tell me what the matter is this instant."

I had known Lee Bang for three months, but he was wearing an expression I had never seen before. My heart grew increasingly fearful with each passing second. Finally, he let out a small sigh and spoke.

"The butterflies have disappeared, sir."

Butterflies? Not people, nor cattle, but butterflies? It was a response I could never have imagined. From Lee Bang's furrowed

THE GOVERNOR'S CASE FILE

brows I could tell this was no practical joke. I continued to watch him wordlessly.

"Sir, there is not a single butterfly to be seen in our entire village. To be honest, the villagers have been whispering about it for several days now, but I figured they were just late in coming out this year. I did not want to needlessly startle you, sir, which is why I have not said anything until this moment. But now... It is the first spring in which not a single butterfly has been sighted anywhere in the village." Lee Bang pressed his hands together.

The law of nature dictates that with the return of spring comes the return of life. Flowers bloom, and birds and bees flitter about. The disappearance of butterflies was not even something I had read about in books.

Lee Bang peered up at me again. I remembered my first weeks here, the whispers of the townsfolk about the young and inexperienced new governor. I knew I had to solve this problem one way or another.

"Come in and tell me more. Am I to believe that there is not a trace of a butterfly anywhere in the entire town?"

Lee Bang scurried into the room and kneeled before me. Having lived in the village much longer than I, he was a valuable messenger delivering the citizens' voices to me. He thought for a moment, then nodded.

"Yes, sir. This has not always been the case, however."

KWON PARK

Of course. I had a fleeting memory of seeing butterflies flying about near this very government office building.

"I believe I too have seen butterflies here before."

"I as well, sir! Many, at that. But these past few days... according to the villagers, it has been the last four days or so that the butterflies have all hidden themselves away."

"Four days?"

"Yes. The first person to tell me was the elder teacher. According to him, the butterflies noticeably decreased in number four days ago then disappeared altogether three days ago. I asked around to the other townspeople, and they all echoed his sentiment."

What had changed in the past four days? I searched my memory, but they had felt like normal spring days. No different from the ones before them.

"Nobody noticed at first," Lee Bang continued. "It was when we heard the children singing that we noticed the butterflies had disappeared."

"Singing?"

"Yes, sir. I haven't heard the song myself, but others say the children's song is somewhere along the line of how the butterflies all flew away, so they can no longer catch them."

The butterflies all flew away, so the children can no longer catch them. They say that sometimes children observe their surroundings more sharply than adults do.

THE GOVERNOR'S CASE FILE

"Let us patrol the vicinity. Get ready to leave."

Lee Bang shot up, following closely behind as I exited the government office building.

The streets were lined with bright green foliage, and off in the distance I could see people working in the fields. On any other day I would have stopped to watch for a while, but on this day my eyes focused only on the flowers. Lee Bang was right. Amongst the plethora of brightly colored flowers there was not a single butterfly to be found. The buzzing of the bees, busy pollinating the flowering trees, filled my ears as my eyes scanned desperately for the familiar sight of a butterfly wing. I knew not where to even begin my investigation.

"So it is true."

"Yes, sir."

My first spring here as governor. A crucial time, in which my leadership can mean the difference between a plentiful and despondent harvest. What mistake had I made in my first three months here that such a strange occurrence plagues this town? Where are the butterflies?

"Honored Governor, sir!" Kim, who had been pulling an ox cart to the street corner, stopped and bowed when he saw me.

"Still working hard, I can see."

KWON PARK

I remembered him from when he had visited the government building to report a problem with his beloved ox. At my words of recognition he produced a wide smile and shook his head.

"It's nothing, sir. I am doing well thanks to you."

A small part of my stress seemed to chip away at his words. That's right. I was sent here to help the villagers. I must not waste any time worrying and focus solely on fixing the matter for my subjects. Kim, who had been guiding his ox to the side of the road so I could pass comfortably, paused and hit his thigh with his hand as if he had realized something.

"Right! Sir. Have you heard the news? They say all the butterflies have disappeared from our little town."

"I am aware. I am on my way now to see about the situation."

"Have you heard anything new?" Lee Bang stepped forward and asked Kim.

"You should ask Farmer Park over there in the cabbage field. He has always hated butterflies due to the caterpillars that eat through his crops every year," Kim responded eagerly.

Yes. Every butterfly was once a caterpillar. It felt like Kim had shone a small sliver of light into the abject darkness. Lee Bang patted Kim's back with a bright smile.

"A fantastic idea! Thank you, Kim."

Kim smiled sheepishly and scratched his head. "I'm just glad to be of help, sir."

THE GOVERNOR'S CASE FILE

I nodded. "I give you my thanks. Come to the government building if you ever have any problems."

Kim bowed several times as I passed him. Now, where was this cabbage field of which he had spoken? Though a small village, we had more than our share of cabbage fields. I stood at the fork in the road, surveying the land that lay ahead. Reading my mind, Lee Bang extended his arm and indicated a direction.

"Park's cabbage field is this way, sir."

"I am fortunate to have such a well-versed administrator as you, Lee Bang."

"I am honored, sir."

I followed his lead. The sun was still high in the sky. If only it were not for this most peculiar case, we could have enjoyed the spring sun with a leisurely walk. Where in the world were the butterflies? It felt as if the heavens were testing me. After some time of walking deep in thought, Park's cabbage field revealed itself in front of my eyes.

"Excuse me! Farmer Park!"

Lee Bang waved his hand. From the middle of the green field, a crouched figure clad in white slowly straightened up. So that is Park. I clasped my hands behind my back and squinted as Park stared at me for several moments, then upon recognizing me, shot up and came running. As he approached, I could see that his coat string was undone, causing the sides of his top to flap about as he ran. He quickly adjusted his appearance, wiped his dirty hands on his clothes, and bowed deeply.

"Honored Governor. To what do I owe the honor of your visit?"

"Are you Park, the cabbage farmer?"

"Yes, sir." He stole short glances at me, half anxious, half curious at my sudden appearance at his field.

Lee Bang stepped up. "I apologize for interrupting your busy day. I just have some questions for you. Have you, by chance, seen any butterflies around here?"

A subtle change came over Park's expression. "Indeed, sir. Many butterflies, at that."

"Is that true? Do they still flutter about your field?"

"Well... I'm not sure when exactly, but I have not seen them these past several days."

Lee Bang looked at me, his face a question mark. So the story is the same in the cabbage field. Lee Bang and I exchanged glances.

Park added, "Sir, to be honest I did not even know about the entire ordeal. Butterflies fly through the sky, and I spend all my time looking down at my cabbage crops."

Lee Bang gestured for him to continue.

"Yesterday, when the sun had just passed its highest point, the elder teacher came to visit."

THE GOVERNOR'S CASE FILE

The elder teacher. The teacher Lee Bang had mentioned earlier. There was no doubt he had already figured out something was amiss.

"He came by and asked when I had last seen a butterfly. I thought about it, and I answered that it had been at least three days. Of course I cannot be sure, as for a farmer such as myself each day is the same as any other. As my gaze is always lowered to the ground, there is a chance I simply missed seeing any that had flown by."

Four days, according to Lee Bang. Three days, according to Park. The timelines were both recent.

Park continued, his eyes full of curiosity. "But this is the time of year when they should be most active! That much I know. Is there a problem with the butterflies, sir?"

I shook my head, all too aware that I had no real information to give him. It was my job to make sure false rumors did not spread among the villagers, causing undue panic.

"There is no issue. I was simply curious, as word has come out about this curious phenomenon. Have you seen caterpillars in your field, then?"

At the mention of caterpillars, Park scowled and shuddered. "Those pesky insects eat through my crops every year. They're killing me! Of course I have seen them. Just as they did last year, they have infested my crops and leave large holes in my cabbage leaves."

KWON PARK

No butterflies, but plenty of caterpillars. How was this possible? As far as I knew, butterflies did not engage in seasonal migrations. I had heard of animals fleeing an area before a natural disaster, but surely there was no such disaster on the horizon.

"There are still caterpillars, sir," Park continued, "as they do not all become butterflies at once."

"Is that so? Your losses must be great."

"Such is the life of a farmer, sir. Those caterpillars are just doing what they must. I go through my cabbage leaves every day and remove as many of them as I can. Although, as the weather has been getting warmer more children have been playing near my field. Perhaps that is why I have seen smaller numbers of caterpillars this spring. Now that I think about it, that is quite unusual."

"I see. Well you still have caterpillars, so do come find me at the government office if any of them turn into butterflies."

"Yes, yes. As you wish, sir! Spend not a minute more worrying about this matter, for I will run right over to you as soon as I see anything."

Lee Bang waited until he was sure I was finished, then gestured for Park to leave. "You may go now, Park."

"I shall be on my way then, sir." Park bowed deeply and walked back to his field. His wife was waiting for him among their crops, her neck craned toward him in curiosity. As I watched their interaction, Lee Bang suddenly stuck his face in front of mine.

THE GOVERNOR'S CASE FILE

"Sir, is this not strange? While the number of caterpillars has indeed decreased, it makes no sense that only the butterflies have completely disappeared."

"Indeed. This is very strange indeed."

"What shall we do, sir?"

"Let us go to the school next. I am sure the elder teacher knows something that we do not."

Lee Bang nodded and stepped in front of me to lead the way. As if realizing something, he turned back around. "When I spoke to him earlier, he had left the school premises, saying he had somewhere to be. I do believe we will not be able to find him at the school nor his residence."

"Somewhere to be?" So he is making the rounds as well. It struck me that his instinct was not to come directly to me with the problem, but to investigate for himself. I wondered if he did not trust me.

"Then let us return to the government office."

Lee Bang bowed slightly and walked behind me. As we trudged through the dirt road, I kept my eyes glued to the sights around me. Where I should have seen butterflies fluttering in the breeze like spring flowers, I saw only air.

Back at the office, I searched through the books in my possession but found only short descriptions of the butterfly and no mention of butterfly disappearances or what to do in such a case.

KWON PARK

My head began to ache. Butterflies pollinate flowers, so the absence of butterflies will surely have a negative impact on the flowers in our village. If something has happened to the butterflies, why, then, are bees flying about as if nothing is the matter? How long could we expect the bees to bear the brunt of spring pollination before the issue gets out of hand?

Through the window, I could see the sky was darkening as the sun made its descent. What was I to tell the royal court about this fiasco? I had not found out a single thing. Gossip is a dangerous thing; if word were to get out and people started whispering that the heavens were testing our king, it would be disastrous.

I called for Lee Bang.

I heard quick footsteps before the door slowly opened. "Did you call for me, sir?"

"Are you close to Park, the cabbage farmer we visited earlier today?"

"Farmer Park, sir?" Lee Bang tilted his head in confusion. "As you saw, he is more of an acquaintance."

"I would like you to go to Park's cabbage field tomorrow and see for yourself what happens to the butterflies right after they undergo metamorphosis."

"All day, sir? Then who will be by your side tomorrow?"

"I shall be fine alone for one day. I plan to visit the school then join you at the field, so do not worry about me."

THE GOVERNOR'S CASE FILE

Lee Bang appeared unconvinced, his brow furrowed in concern. "Sir, perhaps you should call Ye Bang or Gong Bang…"

"They are busy with their own work. You are my hands and feet in this town, and I trust that you will fulfill your duty accordingly."

Lee Bang relented and nodded. I knew he had a difficult day ahead of him in the field. I vowed to acknowledge his troubles once this case was solved.

"You may retire for the day," I said.

"Yes, sir. I will see you tomorrow."

Even after Lee Bang left, I remained unmoving for quite some time. If the newly formed butterflies took to the skies tomorrow without issue, I could close the case as just a short-term commotion. I prayed that would be the case. I got up only when the candle melted completely, snuffing out the light in the room.

At dawn, I got ready to leave and paced the courtyard of my residence, having woken up early after a fitful night of worrying. While the farmers were already hard at work in their fields, it was still too early to visit the school, especially as it also served as the elder teacher's private residence. I peeked over the courtyard wall, standing tiptoe, but I saw no butterflies. I paused, somewhat self-conscious that I was acting like a heartsick man waiting for his lover.

KWON PARK

Fluttering white butterfly, spotted tiger swallowtail.
How high they fly.
Far, far away. For a new home they sway.
Out of our reach. No longer to meet.
Fluttering white butterfly, spotted tiger swallowtail...

I heard the high voices of children singing. Two voices similar in pitch, singing in unison. The song Lee Bang informed me of the day prior. I listened intently to the lyrics. Despite the sad lyrics, the children's voices sounded merry. Did they not know what they were singing? I looked over the fence once again to see their faces, but they had already passed by the building.

I judged that it had reached an appropriate time to visit the school, as the children were walking about the village, and set out. The morning sun had risen rapidly, bathing the town in a bright glow. I wondered if Lee Bang had made it to the cabbage field. I hoped he would find a comfortable spot to sit, out of the harsh sunlight.

I exchanged cheery pleasantries with all those I passed. Everyone mentioned the butterflies, but to my relief nobody seemed panicked.

I thought back to when I had first arrived at this village, how I had heard the elder teacher was highly educated despite residing in such a small town. It was said that he had been so accomplished as to take up public office, and even parents from neighboring towns

THE GOVERNOR'S CASE FILE

would come in person to ask him to teach their children. I realized it would have been prudent of me to visit him sooner, seeing as how he is acknowledged as the town's primary elder, but when I first sent someone to pay my respects the elder teacher had not seemed keen on getting involved with political leaders. I stood in front of his well-decorated front gate, one befitting an aristocrat such as himself, and loudly declared myself.

"Is anyone home?"

After a moment, the door opened slightly at first, then all the way.

"Honored Governor!"

"Is the elder teacher available?"

"Yes, yes, sir. I will tell him you are here. Please come in."

The man left the door wide open and ran in to get the teacher. He looked so much like Lee Bang at that moment that I chuckled. Another interior door opened, and a dignified elderly man emerged.

"Honored Governor. To what do I owe the pleasure?"

"I am here to discuss the matter of the butterflies."

The teacher nodded knowingly. I followed him inside and sat down.

"How much do you know, Teacher? Do you have any inkling of why the butterflies have suddenly disappeared?" I asked.

"I have made every effort to find out myself, but sadly I still know nothing."

I felt disappointed at his answer. Perhaps I had been pinning all my hopes of solving this mystery onto him.

"How did you first hear of the butterflies?"

"I heard my students singing the song one day. The one about the butterflies. Sure enough, when I looked around, the butterflies had disappeared."

"I heard that song myself, just this morning. Do you know who first started singing it?"

"When I asked the children, they all said that they did not know."

I decided to ask the students myself when they showed up to class. The teacher lowered his voice and whispered, as if delivering a secret, "What I have noticed, sir, is that the butterflies actually started disappearing at the same time the children started singing their song."

"That makes sense. The children must have started singing after they noticed the absence of the butterflies."

"No, sir. It was simultaneous. The butterflies did not disappear completely overnight, but the song..."

"So the children must know something, then!"

The teacher nodded, unbothered by my loud outburst. "I asked the children yesterday, but not one of them answered in a satisfying way. They are all remaining silent about who first started singing the song. I do wonder what the story is."

"When do the children arrive for class? I would like to speak to them myself."

The teacher hesitated. "Well, sir, most of the children are still quite young. I fear they may feel nervous in your presence…"

"I have no intention of making them feel anxious. I simply wish to get to the bottom of the matter as quickly as possible." I understood that to the children, their teacher would be a much more comforting presence than the unfamiliar governor, but no matter. Questions needed to be asked.

A long moment of silence ensued. I heard a familiar voice outside.

"Honorable Governor! Please come take a look! I saw it! I saw it!"

Lee Bang was in the school courtyard, stamping his feet and calling out for me. I ran out and saw him gesturing wildly, his face bright and flushed.

"Let us go, sir! I will brief you on our way!"

I forgot all about my yet unfinished conversation with the teacher and hurriedly crammed my feet into my shoes. I turned back to see the teacher nodding and waving at me to go on. I gave a small bow and followed Lee Bang.

"What is it that you have seen? Is there a butterfly flying about?"

"Yes, sir! I saw with my own two eyes a cabbage white flitting leisurely about! However... after that, well, something I could never have imagined happened, sir."

"What is it?" I tamped down the frustration that was rising within me at Lee Bang's dilly-dallying.

"Well... it was Mr. Lee's young son, sir! I saw him capture the butterfly!"

"He captured the butterfly, you say?"

"Yes, sir! Very carefully, at that! He definitely wanted to keep the butterfly alive, it seemed." Lee Bang nodded his head incredulously.

The wind whipped in my face as we approached the cabbage field. I looked around, but I did not see a child.

"Where is the boy?" I asked. I planned to catch him red-handed.

Lee Bang called Farmer Park over. "Over there, sir! He went over there into that mountain!" Park said.

Even at a quick glance, the area to which Park had gestured was a large and dark mountain. A place much too dangerous for a child to enter, even in daylight. I was now consumed with concern for the child as I quickened my pace to a run.

"Sir! I continued watching the child to see what he would do with the butterfly!" Lee Bang huffed, struggling to keep up.

"I understand!" I called back to him. Soon Lee Bang was unable to run any farther, and I headed into the mountain alone. Unlike the bright spring sun that shone outside the forest, the heavily wooded mountain road was dark. I noticed a small section of thicket a small child had clearly made his way through and followed the same path. What a fearless child he was, navigating such a treacherous area alone.

I soon learned how gravely I had underestimated the boy, for I walked for what felt like hours but still saw no trace of him. I feared this chase would come to nothing in the end. Should I go find the boy's father instead? My steps slowed as fatigue set in. I willed my legs to move. I could not leave the child alone so deep in the mountains. Finally, up ahead, I saw a bright beam of sunlight shining among the trees. Had this child truly made it through the entire mountain forest and come out on the other side? That was when I heard the same cheery voice from that morning.

"Brother! Now nobody will ever be able to find any butterflies, right?"

"No, that's not true. We must keep looking around us. There will be new butterflies every day, like this one here."

"Really? How much longer do we need to keep catching butterflies?"

"I don't know. But we can't give up…"

A boy and his younger sister sat leaning against a tree. I approached them briskly.

"You rascals! What are you doing in such a dangerous mountain?"

KWON PARK

I stepped out of the darkness, and blinding sunlight washed over my entire body. My eyes struggled to adjust after having been in the dark for so long. I squeezed my eyes shut and slowly opened them.

"My heavens..." Beyond the scared-looking siblings stretched an endless field of bright yellow canola flowers. It was an unbelievable scene, a gently undulating ocean of flowers covering an entire section of the mountain. They sparkled like yellow silk in the sun. Among the flowers, a horde of butterflies fluttered their wings and filled the air like stars in a bright blue sky. Only in heaven would a scene like this exist. My mouth fell open as I observed the hundreds of colorful butterflies. They were all here. Every last one of them.

"Honored Governor, please forgive us."

"Please forgive us, sir."

The boy fell at my feet, his forehead to the ground, and his sister followed. She began to cry.

I extended my hand. "Stand up, children. We will take care of this matter at the government office. Let us return to town first."

Villagers crowded the office as the two children stood in the courtyard. Though they were indeed a pitiable sight, my job was to distinguish right from wrong and assign the proper consequences.

THE GOVERNOR'S CASE FILE

The sister stood clutching her dirty skirt, thick teardrops plopping silently from her eyes. I gestured to Lee Bang.

"Is it true that you captured all the town butterflies?" he asked the children.

"Yes, sir."

The young boy, older than his sister yet no older than ten, nodded.

"And are you the ones who started the song that all the children were singing?" I asked.

The boy nodded once again, wordlessly this time. His face displayed a determination rare for children his age.

"Explain yourself," I said.

The boy remained silent for some time, as if in protest. Finally, he drew in a breath and spoke. "I sang the song to let the villagers know that the butterflies had disappeared."

"Did the villagers need to know about the butterflies' disappearance?"

"Yes, sir."

"What is the reason?"

"So nobody else would catch any butterflies."

The story was going in circles. Just like the village children who refused to answer the teacher's questions, the boy in front of me seemed reticent to explain his true motive. Whispers soon grew louder near the office gate. Out of nowhere, a man and woman shoved their way through the crowd to appear before me. Their clothes were worn and dirty. Their agitated eyes scanned the courtyard before landing on their children, whom they held in their arms briefly before falling to their knees on the dirt. They begged for mercy with hoarse voices.

"Honorable Governor. This is the deed of two ignorant children. They know nothing, sir. Please have mercy."

"If there is to be a punishment, I will receive it as their father. Please release the children, Honorable Governor sir."

Watching her parents wringing their hands and begging for mercy on their knees, the girl let out a loud wail. The onlookers sighed at the pitiable sight. This was not what I had wanted at all. I stood up, taken aback at how the events were unfolding and the unmistakable fact that I must look like quite the villain in everyone's eyes.

"Please, everyone, settle down. Our Governor is not a heartless man. You all know this, so please settle down." Lee Bang helped the man and woman up. He gave the daughter, now holding tightly onto her mother's skirt, a gentle pat on the back and looked up at me with the look of a man who had been through hell and back.

"We simply want to know why the children took all the butterflies, that is all. Do you know the reason?" I asked the parents.

They shook their heads. There was no deception on their faces.

THE GOVERNOR'S CASE FILE

"No, sir. We do not know. We heard the rumors just like everyone else, but we had no idea our children were involved."

I peered at the boy. His mouth was shut tightly, his face full of despair.

"Why did you hide the butterflies?" I asked again.

The courtyard fell silent as the villagers waited for the boy's answer. At that moment the girl stopped her sobbing, wiped the tears from her face, and declared in a clear voice, "Because our parents might split up!"

Everyone stared at the children, unable to make heads or tails of her response. They took the butterflies to stop their parents from splitting up. The connection between the two eluded me. At her outburst, the girl's brother squeezed his eyes shut as if bracing for the worst. Slowly, the villagers began whispering.

"A few nights ago, I overheard our parents talking," the boy finally said. "They said that if things continued this way, they will have to exchange butterflies to prevent our family from starving to death."

The crowd fell silent.

"At first, I did not know what they meant. But when I continued listening, I was able to figure out that exchanging butterflies means our family will no longer be together."

So that was the story. I exhaled sharply. Loud puffs could be heard throughout the crowd, but otherwise everyone was silent.

KWON PARK

In his innocence, the boy had equated the traditional method of finalizing a divorce—exchanging pieces of clothing in the shape of a butterfly's wings, dubbed "exchanging butterflies"—with exchanging live butterflies.

"My parents have a good relationship. They have no land, but they respect each other and care for my sister and me. I felt it was wrong for them to split up because of poverty. As their son, it was my duty to stop them. I wished to hide away all the butterflies until I grew into a man and could help them keep the promises they made to each other at their wedding."

The boy clenched his fists, fighting back tears. His mother wept silently while his father stared at him, his expression unreadable.

"That is why I hid the butterflies. If there were no more butterflies in the village, my parents would be unable to carry out their divorce. There were more butterflies than I expected, so I did get some help from my friends. But it was my idea, and my idea only. They have done nothing wrong, only suffering to help a friend."

My heart ached for the boy. How tragic it is when a child must grow up so early in life.

"I spread the song so my parents would know there were no butterflies to exchange. To be honest, I learned from the elder teacher yesterday that the butterfly is an important insect. I felt guilty, but I could not stop. I swear to you, I did not harm a single butterfly. I released them all in the flower fields that you, Honorable

THE GOVERNOR'S CASE FILE

Governor, saw today. I knew it would be hard for the butterflies to make their way back to the village through the dark mountain woods, so I released them where there were plenty of flowers for them to feast upon. I know I have committed a grave sin, sir. Please forgive me."

The boy's words flowed out of his mouth like water out of a broken faucet. His cheeks glowed red as he loosened his fists and hung his head.

"The butterflies your parents intended to exchange are not live butterflies, but cloth ones," I said gently.

The boy raised his head and stared at me.

I continued. "These cloth butterflies are exchanged as a symbol of divorce. I now understand your true intentions, but I cannot ignore the actions you have taken to capture all the butterflies in our village."

The boy's eyes filled with tears. I rushed to announce my ruling.

"In consideration of the facts of this case, which are that you did not harm the butterflies but released them in a safe location, I order you to return them all to the village."

The boy's eyes widened. Yes. This young child was not at fault.

"In my life I have never seen a child so filled with filial duty and love. In your young age you have demonstrated a commitment to keeping your family together, and for this I shall help your parents avoid divorce."

KWON PARK

The boy stood still, unable to comprehend my words. His father grabbed him and wrapped his arms around him. Safely in his father's arms, the boy let out a sob. Ever so strong and mature until that moment, he was still only a child. The onlookers exclaimed in relief, embracing one another and offering congratulations to the family. Emotion threatened to overcome me when I glanced down at Lee Bang and witnessed him wiping away his tears with his sleeve.

So the boy and girl, with the help of their friends, carefully transported the butterflies from the canola flower field back to our village. To the children I provided rice and coins, and to the parents I bestowed a small tract of land in acknowledgment of their part in raising such devoted and dutiful children. No longer will that family worry about splitting up due to poverty. Your Royal Highness, there is an old saying that as sandalwood is fragrant even as a seed leaf, exemplary character displays itself early in life. I have not yet come across a child so filled with filial duty. I am confident that the boy will grow into a fine man, a man who will one day be your loyal subject. I humbly ask that you provide him with the opportunity to prove his worth in the larger world outside of his small village.

THE GOVERNOR'S CASE FILE

The king chuckled. "This is from Governor Park in Gangwon Province, you say?"

"Yes, Your Majesty."

"What an amusing and heartwarming occurrence. Call Governor Park and this child to the Court immediately. I wish to meet with them."

"Certainly, Your Majesty."

As the eunuch shuffled away, the king looked back down at the document in his hands. He unfolded the scroll he had just finished reading and started again, a smile spreading across his lips.

사또의 사건일지

박권

나비와북
Nabiwabook

사또의 사건일지

　소중한 내 고을. 비록 산골인 데다 작은 마을이긴 해도 여기까지 오기 위해 많은 고생을 했지. 몇 없는 백성들도 참 순박하고 이렇다 할 커다란 사고도 없다. 한겨울에 부임해 벌써 봄 기운이 찾아왔나 했더니 고을이 온통 옅은 녹색으로 물들었다. 담벼락 위로 슬그머니 내다보이는 커다란 산들은 보고만 있어도 마음 한쪽이 뿌듯하게 차오르는 듯했다. 만족스러움을 한껏 담은 숨을 내쉬며 머름에 팔을 걸치고 창을 내다봤다. 항상 곁에 붙어 있던 이방도 잠시 쉬러 갔는지 보이지 않고. 미시에서 신시가 넘어가는 시간 동안 큰 소리 한 번 나지 않았다. 오늘 유독 평화롭구나. 차라도 한잔 내릴까. 일전에 조카님께 받은 당과가 아직 남았을 텐데.

박권

"사또 나으리!"

이런. 입이 방정이군. 호랑이도 제 말 하면 온다더니. 멀리서 들리는 커다란 목소리와 분주한 발소리에 잠시 벗어두었던 전립을 들어 머리에 얹었다. 호들갑 떠는 자가 아니거늘 어찌 이리 급하게 달려온단 말인가. 무슨 일이라도 생긴 걸까 걱정이 몰려들었다. 버석한 마당에 흙먼지를 일으키며 도착한 이방이 이쪽을 올려다보며 눈치를 살폈다.

"무슨 일이라도 생겼는가."

"그게…"

당장이라도 말을 쏟아낼 기세로 달려온 것이 무색하게 우물쭈물 쉽사리 입을 열지 못하는 그를 가만히 내려다보았다.

"어서 고해 보거라."

부임한 지 석 달이나 지났건만 이방은 한 번도 본 적이 없는 표정을 짓고 있었다. 시간을 끌수록 조마조마해지는 마음을 견디기 힘들어 헛기침을 하면서 이방을 채근했다. 그가 작게 한 숨을 쉬더니 마지못해 운을 떼었다.

"나비가 사라졌습니다."

나비? 사람도 아니고 가축도 아닌 나비? 전혀 예상하지 못한 말에 당황스러워 나도 모르게 되물으려던 걸 참았다. 한껏 처진 눈썹을 보면 농이 아닌 건 확실한데. 대답 없이 바라만 보고 있자 눈을 이리저리 굴리던 이방이 안절부절못하던 손을 공손하게 모으고 덧붙였다. "고을에 나비가 보이지 않습니다.

사또의 사건일지

실은 며칠 전부터 마을에서 이야기가 나오고 있었지만 금년 조금 늦어지는 것뿐이겠지, 조금만 더 기다리면 나오겠지 싶어 말씀드리지 않았습니다. 헌데 이리 약속이라도 한 듯 나비가 싹 사라진 봄은 처음이라…."

　만물이 살아나는 봄이 오면 꽃이 피어나고 나비와 벌이 날아다니는 것이 자연의 이치이거늘. 나비가 날아다니지 않는다니 이런 건 서적에서 읽어본 적도 없다. 이방이 다시 내 눈치를 살폈다. 마을에서도 이야기가 나오고 있다지만 이방이 이리 고할 정도면 소문이 이제 막 시작된 수준을 넘어 이미 파다하게 퍼져 있을 텐데. 처음 부임했을 때 젊은 사또가 왔다며 수군대던 백성들의 얼굴이 휙 스쳐 지나갔다. 이 문제는 어떻게든 해결해 보여야 한다.

　"이리 올라와 자세히 고해보게. 나비가 아예 날아다니지 않는다는 말인가."

　이방이 허둥지둥 방 안으로 들어와 앞에 꿇어앉았다. 이 고을에 오래 있던지라 백성들의 목소리를 생생히 전해주는 내 귀와 같은 자였다. 그가 잠시 기억을 되짚더니 고개를 끄덕였다. "예. 허나 처음부터 나비가 없던 건 아니었습니다."

　그럴 것이다. 얼마 전까지 관아 담벼락을 넘나들며 팔랑팔랑 날던 나비를 본 기억은 똑똑하다. "나도 나비를 본 적이 있네."

박권

"저도 보았습니다. 그것도 꽤 많이 보았습죠. 헌데 요 며칠… 마을 사람들 말을 모아보면 대략 나흘 사이 고을에 있던 나비가 전부 자취를 감추었습니다."

"나흘?"

"예. 처음 제게 귀띔을 한 건 동네 훈장 어르신입니다. 나흘 전부터 나비가 눈에 띄게 줄어들더니 사흘 전부터 전혀 보이지 않는다는 겁니다. 이야기를 듣고 다른 자들에게 물었더니 보이지 않는다고들 했습니다."

나흘 사이에 대체 무슨 일이 있었단 말인가. 기억을 더듬어 봐도 요 며칠은 평소와 다름없이 봄기운이 완연한 평범한 날들이었다.

"처음에는 다들 눈치채지 못했습니다. 헌데 아이들이 노래를 부르는 걸 듣고 가만 보니 나비가 전부 사라졌다는 겁니다."

"노래?"

"예. 저도 전해 들은 거라 자세히는 모르지만 나비가 날아갔다, 그래서 잡을 수 없다, 그런 내용이라고 합니다요."

나비가 날아갔다. 그래서 잡을 수 없다. 지금 상황 그대로였다. 아이들의 관찰력은 때때로 어른보다 날카롭다더니. 나비가 사라진 걸 진작 알고 노래까지 만든 상황이로구나. 한발 늦었군. "순찰을 돌아야겠다. 나갈 준비를 하거라."

사또의 사건일지

　이방이 벌떡 자리에서 일어났다. 문 곁에서 비켜서는 그를 지나쳐 관아를 나섰다.

　길 주변으로 초록색 풀들이 파릇파릇하게 자리하고 저 멀리 논과 밭 근처에는 백성들이 허리가 굽어가는 줄 모르고 바삐 움직이고 있었다. 평소 순찰이라면 이런 모습들을 한참 눈에 담았겠지만 지금은 시선이 온통 꽃 근처로 향했다. 이방의 말이 사실이었다. 봄을 알리기라도 하듯 흐드러지게 핀 꽃 주변에 나비는 한 마리도 보이지 않았다. 꽃나무 근처를 지나갈 때면 바쁘게 날아다니는 벌의 날갯짓 소리가 귓가에 윙윙 울렸지만 애타게 찾는 나비는 날개 끄트머리도 찾기 힘들었다. 어디서부터 조사를 해야 하는지, 어떻게 접근해야 하는 문제인지 감조차 잡히지 않았다. 막막한 나머지 절로 나오려는 한숨을 꾹꾹 눌러 참았다.
　"정말이로구나."
　"예에…."
　부임하고 첫 봄. 풍작과 흉작을 가르는 중요한 시기. 짧은 석 달 사이에 내가 무언가 잘못한 것이라도 있었단 말인가. 어찌 나비가 보이질 않아.
　"아이고, 사또 나으리."
　모퉁이 앞쪽에서 소달구지를 끌고 오던 김 씨가 나를 보더니 걸음을 멈추고 고개를 조아렸다.

박권

"그래, 고생이 많구나."

애지중지 기르던 소에 문제가 생겨 관아를 찾은 적이 있는 자다. 그를 기억하는 듯한 내 말에 환하게 웃으며 고개를 가로젓는다.

"아휴, 아닙니다요. 나으리 덕분에 이리 잘 살고 있구먼요."

갑작스레 들이닥친 나비 문제로 가득하던 근심이 조금은 걷힌 느낌이 들었다. 그래. 나는 이 백성들에게 도움을 주는 사람이다. 걱정에 빠져 있을 시간은 없어. 문제를 해결하는 데 집중 해야만 한다. 내가 편히 지나갈 수 있도록 소를 길가로 몰던 김 씨가 허벅지를 손바닥으로 탁 쳤다.

"참, 나으리. 이야기 들으셨습니까요. 요 며칠 사이 마을에 나비가 전부 사라졌다는구먼요."

"알고 있다. 마침 그 문제 때문에 나비를 확인하러 나온 길이다."

"뭐, 들은 거라도 있는감?"

뒤에 서있던 이방이 내 대신 한 발 나서며 그에게 물었다. 김 씨가 냉큼 덧붙였다.

"아, 그러면 저어기 배추밭에 있는 박 씨에게 물어보시는 게 어떻습니까요? 매년 나비 애벌레놈들 때문에 골머리를 썩던 사람입니다요."

옳다구나. 그래, 나비가 되려면 애벌레를 거쳐야지. 실마리 하나 보이지 않던 암담함 속에서 한줄기 빛을 찾은

사또의 사건일지

느낌이었다. 이방도 마찬가지였는지 환하게 웃으며 김 씨의 등을 두드렸다. "고맙네! 좋은 귀띔을 해줬네 그려!"

"아휴, 저 같은 게 도움이 되었다니 다행이구먼요."

김 씨가 쏟아지는 칭찬에 민망한지 웃으면서 뒷머리를 긁적였다.

"고맙구나. 일이 생기면 언제든 다시 찾아오거라."

연신 감사를 전하며 허리를 숙이는 김 씨와 달구지를 지나쳐 길을 걸었다. 헌데, 저어기 배추 밭이 어딘지 알 길이 있나. 작은 고을이긴 해도 산골이라 배추밭이 한둘이 아닐 텐데. 갈림길에 서서 밭 근처를 빙 둘러보는 사이 이방도 고개를 두리번거리더니 한쪽 팔을 펼쳐 길을 안내했다.

"나으리, 박 씨 배추밭은 이쪽입니다."

"자네처럼 유능한 이방이 있어 참 다행이야."

"그렇게 말씀해 주시니 몸 둘 바를 모르겠습니다."

고을 지리를 구석구석까지 잘 알고 있는 그의 안내를 따라 바삐 걸음을 옮겼다. 해가 길어져서 그런지 날은 여전히 화창했다. 나비가 사라졌다는 중대한 사건만 아니면 여유롭게 걸으며 이 봄볕을 즐겼을 터인데. 한두 마리도 아닌 나비 떼가 전부 어디로 갔단 말인가. 하늘이 나를 시험하기라도 하시는 건가. 근심에 잠겨 걷다 보니 저만치 앞에 배추밭이 가까워졌다.

"어이! 이 보시게! 박 씨!"

박권

 이방이 한쪽 손을 들어 흔들면서 목소리를 높였다. 녹색 밭 한가운데서 하얀 공처럼 웅크리듯 몸을 숙이고 있던 누군가가 고개를 들었다. 저자가 박 씨로구나. 뒷짐을 지고 눈을 가늘게 떠 밭을 들여다보고 있자 한참 마주보던 남자가 벌떡 일어나더니 황급히 밭을 가로질러 달려왔다. 가까워지자 다 풀린 옷고름이 옆구리에 위태롭게 매달려 흔들리고 있는 게 보였다. 밭에서 빠져나온 그가 길로 성큼 올라왔다. 옷매무새를 급하게 정리하더니 흙이 묻은 손을 옷에 삭삭 비벼 먼지를 털어내고 꾸벅 고개를 숙인다.

 "사또 나으리. 예까지 어인 일로 오셨습니까요."
 "자네가 배추 농사를 짓는다는 박 씨인가."
 "예에. 맞습니다."
 갑작스러운 방문에 당황스러움 반, 호기심 반이 담긴 시선이 힐끔힐끔 내 쪽으로 향했다.
 "바쁠 텐데 미안하네 그려. 자네 혹시 이 주변에서 나비 봤는감?"
 이방이 단도직입적으로 물었다. 박 씨의 표정이 미묘하게 변했다. "봤습죠. 그것도 꽤 많이 봤습니다요."
 "그래? 지금도 잘 날아다니는가?"
 "그게… 정확히 언제인지는 기억나지 않습니다만… 요 며칠 사이 보이지 않았습니다요."

사또의 사건일지

이방이 이제 어쩌면 좋겠냐는 듯 이쪽을 돌아보았다. 배추밭에서도 나비가 사라진지 얼마 지나지 않았다는 거로군. 시선을 주고받는 우리를 보던 박 씨가 슬그머니 덧붙였다.

"실은 저도 몰랐습니다요. 나비야 봄이면 하늘에 날아댕기는 거고 저는 배추를 살핀다고 땅만 보고 있으니께요."

이방이 계속 말해보라며 손짓을 했다. 그 몸짓에 박 씨가 힘을 얻어 이야기를 술술 풀었다. "어제 해가 머리 꼭대기에서 조금 내려갔을 즈음인가… 훈장님이 오셨습니다요."

이방이 말했던 훈장 이야기다. 벌써 다녀갔다니. 이 사태에 대해 진작 눈치챈 것이 분명하군.

"오셔서는 나비를 마지막으로 본 게 언제냐고 물어보시기에 한참 생각을 해보니께 사흘은 넘은 것 같았습죠. 농사꾼에게는 매일매일이 비슷하다 보니 정확하진 않습니다요. 게다가 내내 고개를 숙이고 있어 나비가 날아다녔지만 놓친 적도 있을 수 있구요."

이방이 전해온 건 나흘. 마을 외곽에 있는 배추밭은 사흘. 둘 다 꽤 최근이다.

"요즘 한껏 날아 댕길 때긴 헌데… 요 근래 안 보이는 게 무슨 문제라도 있습니까요?"

박 씨가 호기심 가득한 눈으로 물었다. 아무런 정보도 없는 마당에 허튼소리는 할 수가 없어 고개를 저었다. 괜히

박권

 안 좋은 이야기가 돌 빌미를 줄 필요는 없지. 백성들이 불안에 떨기 시작하면 걷잡을 수 없게 될지도 모른다.
 "말이 나와 물어보는 게지 큰일은 아니네. 그보다 나비를 봤다면 애벌레도 제대로 있었는가?"
 애벌레라는 말만 들어도 싫은지 박 씨가 인상을 쓰며 진저리를 쳤다.
 "어휴, 그놈들 매년 배추를 갉아먹어서 죽겠구만요. 있었습니다. 예년하고 다를 거 없이 배춧잎에 구멍을 아주 숭숭 뚫어놨습죠."
 애벌레는 있었고 변태까지 마쳐 잘 날아다니던 나비가 갑자기 사라지다니. 이럴 수가 있단 말인가. 나비가 철을 맞춰 이동한다는 이야기는 들어본 적도 없는데. 커다란 천재지변이 일어나기 직전 동물들이 움직인다는 건 들어본 적이 있지만 이런 태평성대이거늘.
 "애벌레는 지금도 있습니다요. 한 번에 다 같이 나비가 되는 게 아닌지라…."
 "그래? 피해가 크겠구나."
 "어쩌겠습니까. 지들도 살겠다고 기어 나오는디. 이파리를 뒤지면서 쫓아내고는 있습니다요. 아, 그러고 보니 요즘은 날이 풀리면서 아이들이 밭 근처에서 놀아서 그런가 평소보다 애벌레가 적어 쫓아내는 수고를 덜고는 있습니다요. 허어, 지금 생각해보니께 신기하구만요."

사또의 사건일지

 "그런가. 그래도 애벌레가 아주 없는 건 아니니 밭일하느라 바쁘겠지만 나비가 다시 날아다니기 시작하면 관아로 와서 알려주게나."
 "아휴. 나으리 말씀이면 바로 달려가겠습니다요. 걱정 딱 붙들어 매셔요."
 이방이 잠시 내 뒷말을 기다리더니 이야기가 끝난 걸 눈치채고 박 씨에게 손짓을 했다. "이제 가봐도 되네."
 "그럼 다시 가보겠습니다요."
 박 씨가 허리를 깊게 숙여 인사하고 밭 안쪽으로 향했다. 저 멀리 박 씨의 아내로 보이는 자가 무슨 일이 있었던 건지 궁금한 듯 땡볕 아래 목을 쭉 빼고 그를 기다리고 있었다. 둘을 가만히 보고 있는데 이방이 그 앞을 불쑥 가로막고 얼굴을 디밀었다.
 "나으리, 이상하지 않습니까? 애벌레가 예년보다 적기는 해도 아주 없는 게 아닌데 나비만 사라졌다는 건 말이 되지 않습니다."
 "그래. 참 해괴한 일이로구나."
 "어찌해야 할까요?"
 "우선 서당에 가서 훈장을 직접 만나 봐야겠다. 무언가 알고 있는 게 틀림없어."
 동의한다며 고개를 끄덕이고 앞장서 서당으로 향하려던 이방이 아차 하는 표정으로 뒤돌았다. "아까 저와 이야기를

박권

나누고 어디 갈 곳이 있다고 하면서 자리를 비웠습니다. 서당이나 댁에 가도 자리에 없을 듯합니다만….”

"자리에 없다?"

이 배추밭에도 다녀간 걸 보면 다른 곳도 살펴보는 중인가 보군. 이상함을 눈치챘음에도 불구하고 내게 고하러 오는 게 아니라 직접 문제를 살펴본다는 말인데. 나를 믿지 못하는 건가. "그럼 우선 다시 관아로 돌아가자꾸나."

이방이 가벼운 목례와 함께 뒤로 따라붙었다. 자박자박 흙길에 한 발을 디딜 때마다 눈을 한 번 돌려 고을을 살폈지만 따뜻한 봄 한가운데 하늘의 꽃처럼 보여야 할 나비는 온데간데 없었다.

관아로 돌아와 급한대로 가지고 있는 서적을 여럿 넘겨보았지만 나비라는 곤충에 대한 설명이 짧게 나올 뿐 나비가 사라지는 이유나 사라졌을 경우 해결책에 대한 내용은 눈곱만큼도 적혀 있지 않았다. 절로 머리가 아파왔다. 나비는 꽃의 수분을 돕는 곤충이니 나비의 부재는 곧 수분의 부재로 이어진다. 허나 벌은 멀쩡히 날아다니고. 벌에게 수분을 맡기면… 당장 문제는 없겠지만 나비가 사라진 이유가 다른 문제를 더 일으킬 수도 있는 노릇이니 손을 놓고 있을 수는 없다.

사또의 사건일지

답답한 마음에 창 너머를 바라보자 해가 언제 기운 건지 어둑어둑한 하늘이 나를 반겼다. 조정에 무어라 고한단 말인가. 아직 아무것도 밝혀내지 못했다. 소문이 잘못 흘러가 하늘이 전하를 시험하신다는 이야기가 돌기라도 하면 큰일이다. 역시 내 선에서 해결하는 게 맞아. 이렇게 아무 조치도 취하지 않은 채 시간이 흘러가는 걸 보고만 있을 수는 없다.

"게 있는가."

나무 바닥 위를 분주히 걸어오는 소리가 들리더니 문이 조심스레 열렸다. "찾으셨습니까."

"자네 낮에 그 배추밭에 있던 박 씨하고는 가까운가?"

"박 씨요?"

이방이 영문을 모르겠다는 표정으로 고개를 갸웃거렸다. "보셨다시피 적당히 아는 사이입니다."

내가 나고 자란 곳으로는 부임할 수 없어 이런 생경한 곳에 왔으니 이방의 도움이 절실했다. "그럼 내일 자네가 박 씨의 밭에 가서 막 변태를 끝낸 나비들이 어찌 되는지 보고 오게."

"예? 하루 종일 말씀이십니까? 그럼 나으리 곁은 누가 지킵니까."

"하루쯤이야 괜찮네. 내일 서당에 가보고 금세 밭으로 갈테니 너무 걱정하지 말게."

박권

　안심시키려는 말을 듣고도 영 마음이 놓이지 않는지 이방의 표정이 어두웠다. "예방이나 공방을 부르는 건 어떠하신지…."
　"그들은 저마다 일이 있고 자네는 내 수족이나 다름없지 않은가. 잘 해줄 거라 믿네."
　응? 하며 어깨를 두드리자 이방은 마지못해 알겠다며 고개를 끄덕인다. 내내 밭에 나가 있으려면 꽤나 애를 먹을 텐데. 나비 실종 사건을 해결하고 나면 고생을 한 번쯤 알아줘야겠군. "오늘은 이만 들어가 보게."
　"예. 내일 뵙겠습니다."
　이방이 가고 나서도 쉽게 자리에서 일어날 수가 없었다. 지금까지 변태를 끝낸 나비들은 사라졌지만 내일 새롭게 날아다닐 것들이 잘 남아 있는다면 요 며칠 간의 소동 정도로 끝낼 수 있다. 제발 문제없이 지나갈 수 있었으면. 결국 초가 다 타 물러지고 나서야 자리에서 일어났다.

　새벽이슬을 맞을 즈음이면 농사일을 하는 자들은 한참 일을 하고 있을 시간이지만 서당에 방문하기에는 아직 이른 시간이다. 근심이 온몸에 자리 잡고 있어 그런지 눈이 일찍 떠져 외출 준비까지 끝냈지만 마당을 서성일 수밖에 없었다. 혹시 몰라 까치발을 들고 내다본 어슴푸레 한 담장 밖에 나비는 없었다. 마치 정인을 기다리기라도 하는 모양새군.

사또의 사건일지

이게 뭐 하는 짓이람. "팔랑팔랑 흰나비, 알록달록 호랑나비. 하늘 높이 날아가네. 멀리멀리 새 집을 찾아. 이제는 잡을 수 없어. 만날 수 없네. 팔랑팔랑 흰나비, 알록달록 호랑나비…"

까치발을 풀고 뒷짐을 지는 순간 밖에서 높은 목소리가 들려왔다. 비슷한 목소리 둘이 노래를 부르고 있었다. 어제 이방이 고했던 그 노래인가 보군. 가사를 다 들어보자 정말 사라진 나비에 대한 노래였다. 이별을 그린 노래임에도 불구하고 즐거운 듯한 아이들의 노랫소리는 명랑하기 그지없었다. 뜻을 모르고 부르는 걸까. 부지런한 아이들의 얼굴을 확인하기 위해 다시 담장 밖을 내다보았지만 바쁘게 걸어가고 있던 건지 이미 사라지고 없었다.

둘 뿐이긴 해도 아이들이 돌아다니는 시간이라면 슬슬 서당에 가도 괜찮을 듯했다. 아침 해는 생각보다 빠른 속도로 떠올라 벌써 주변이 환하게 빛나기 시작했다. 이방은 배추밭으로 잘 갔을까. 이른 시간부터 고생깨나 하겠군. 볕을 피해 편히 앉아 있을 자리라도 있으면 좋으련만. 마을에 딱 하나 있는 서당으로 가는 길 내내 마주치는 자들이 반갑게 인사를 해왔다. 끝에 한 마디를 꼭 덧붙이는 걸 보면 나비가 사라진 걸 대부분이 알고는 있지만 크게 신경 쓰는 느낌은 들지 않았다. 걱정했던 것만큼 쉽게 동요하지 않는 게 참 다행이었다.

박권

그러고 보니 부임 후 서당에 가는 건 처음인데. 처음 부임했을 당시 들려오던 이야기에 따르면 작은 고을임에도 불구하고 서당에 있는 훈장이라는 자의 학식이 꽤 높은 듯했다. 그저 글을 조금 읽을 줄 아는 자가 아니고 실제 벼슬에도 올랐었다고도 하고 옆 고을에서 자식에게 공부를 시키고 싶어 하는 부모가 찾아오기도 한다고 했다. 마을의 어르신 격인 자니 진작 얼굴을 봐 두는 게 좋았을지도 모르지만 처음 사람을 보냈을 때 권력과 어울리고 싶지 않아 하는 느낌을 받아 이제야 만나게 되었다. 양반집인 만큼 구색을 잘 갖춘 대문 앞에 서서 목소리를 높였다.

"이리 오너라."

잠시 서 있자 안쪽에서 문이 빠끔히 열리더니 이내 활짝 젖혔다. "아이고, 사또 나으리."

"훈장님 자리에 있으신가."

"예에. 아뢰겠습니다. 들어오시지요."

문을 활짝 열어두고 훈장을 부르러 헐레벌떡 달려가는 뒷모습이 어쩐지 이방과 닮아 웃음이 나왔다. 안쪽에 있던 문이 벌컥 열리며 안에서 지긋하지만 위엄 있어 보이는 노인이 나왔다.

"사또 나으리. 예까지 어인 일로…."

"나비에 대한 이야기를 나누러 왔습니다."

사또의 사건일지

내 말을 들은 훈장이 올 것이 왔다는 표정을 지었다. 그의 안내대로 안쪽으로 들어가 자리에 앉자마자 길게 끌 필요 없이 질문을 던졌다.

"훈장님은 어디까지 알고 계십니까. 나비가 어찌 사라졌는지 짐작이 가는 데라도 있습니까."

맞은편에 앉은 훈장이 어두운 표정으로 고개를 저었다.

"백방으로 수소문을 해보았지만 아무것도 찾지 못했습니다."

믿는 구석이었던 그의 입에서 모르겠다는 이야기가 나오자 눈앞이 캄캄해졌다. "그럼… 처음 나비가 사라졌다는 건 어찌 알았습니까."

"글공부를 하러 온 아이들이 부르는 노래를 듣고 살펴보니 정말 나비가 사라져 있었습니다."

"그 동요라면 저도 오늘 이른 아침 들었습니다. 누가 시작했는지는 알고 계십니까?"

"제가 아이들에게 물었을 때는 하나같이 다들 모른다고 답하더이다."

오늘 글공부를 하러 아이들이 모이면 다시 한번 물어봐야겠군. 생각에 잠긴 나를 바라보던 훈장이 비밀을 이야기하듯 목소리를 죽이고 덧붙였다.

"헌데 가만히 기억을 더듬어보니 아이들 사이에서 노래가 돌 즈음 나비가 사라졌습니다."

박권

"나비가 사라진 걸 알고 부르기 시작한 노래일 테니 당연하지 않습니까."

"아니지요. 거의 동시에 일어났단 말입니다. 짧은 시간 사이 나비가 사라진 건 맞지만 하루아침에 전부 자취를 감춘 건 아님에도 불구하고…"

"아이들이 뭔가를 알고 있겠군!"

나도 모르게 말허리를 자르고 큰 소리까지 냈건만 아랑곳하지 않은 훈장이 고개를 끄덕였다. "어제 아이들에게 물었지만 어느 누구도 속 시원하게 말하지 않았습니다. 노래를 누가 처음 시작했는지 약속이라도 한 듯 함구하고 있습니다. 대체 어떤 사정이 있는 건지, 참."

"아이들이 언제쯤 공부하러 서당에 모입니까. 직접 물어야겠습니다."

"아직 어린 아이들이 대부분이라 놀랄 터인데…"

"아이들을 다그칠 생각은 없습니다. 다만 하루빨리 이 문제를 해결하고 싶습니다."

아이들에게는 관아에 가야 만날 수 있는 나보다 글공부를 봐주는 훈장이 훨씬 편할 테니 그의 협조가 간절했다. 한동안 침묵이 이어졌다. 그때 밖에서 익숙한 목소리가 들렸다.

"사또 나으리! 나와 보십시오! 봤습니다! 봤어요!"

사또의 사건일지

밭에 보낸 이방이 훈장 댁 마당에서 발을 동동 구르며 애타게 나를 찾고 있었다. 놀라 달려 나가니 얼굴이 환하게 핀 이방이 허둥지둥 손짓을 했다.

"어서 저와 가시지요! 가면서 설명 드리겠습니다!"

아직 훈장과 이야기가 다 끝나지 않았지만 재촉하는 이방의 기세가 엄청나 나도 모르게 신에 발을 구겨 넣었다. 뒤를 돌아보니 따라 나온 훈장이 어서 가보라는 듯 양손을 어정쩡하게 내 밀고 고개를 끄덕이고 있었다. 다녀와서 마저 이야기를 해야겠군. 그에게 가벼운 목례를 한 뒤 벌써 대문을 넘어간 이방을 따라 바삐 걸음을 옮겼다.

"무얼 봤다는 겐가. 나비가 날아다니고 있어?"

"예! 그 하얀 배추흰나비가 여유롭게 나는 걸, 어휴, 제 두 눈으로 똑똑히 봤습니다! 헌데… 그 다음에 정말, 휴! 생각지도 못한 일이 일어나서….'

"무슨 일?"

사람 애간장을 태우듯 한 번에 속 시원히 말하지 않는 바람에 차오르는 숨을 막고 물었다. "이 씨네 어린 아들놈이 그, 그 나비를 잡지 뭡니까!"

"무어라? 나비를 잡아?"

"예에! 그것도 조심스레! 생포하더이다!"

이방도 기가 막힌다면서 고개를 끄덕였다. 빠른 속도로 거의 뛰다시피 걷는 바람에 숨이 턱턱 막혔다. 저만치 앞에

박권

배추밭이 보였다. 서둘러 두리번거렸지만 아이는 보이지 않았다. "아이는?"

현장을 덮쳐야 추궁을 할 텐데. 이방을 보자 이방이 손을 들어 박 씨를 불렀다. "저쪽! 저어쪽 산 입구로 들어갔습니다요!"

박 씨가 가리키는 곳을 휙 돌아보자 한눈에 봐도 커다랗고 어두컴컴한 산이 떡하니 자리 잡고 있었다. 대낮이긴 해도 호랑이라도 나오면 어찌하려고 아이가 그리로 들어갔단 말인가. 나비도 중요했지만 홀로 산에 들어간 아이가 걱정되어 이제는 달릴 수밖에 없었다.

"나으리! 아이가 나비를 어찌하느라 보려고 일부러 지켜보기만 했습니다!"

"알겠네!"

기진맥진해 더 이상 달릴 수 없는 이방을 두고 홀로 아이를 찾기 위해 산속으로 들어갔다. 해가 내리쬐고 있는 바깥과 달리 나무가 우거져 어두컴컴한 산속에는 길이라고 부를 만한 것도 없었다. 불행 중 다행인지 수풀을 헤치고 들어간 자리가 어렴풋이 남아 겨우 아이가 간 방향을 확인하고 앞으로 나아갈 수 있었다. 아무리 철없는 어린아이라지만 겁도 없군.

그래. 어린아이. 조그마한 게 가봤자 얼마나 가겠어, 하고 얕잡아봤지만 얼마나 깊게 들어간 건지 한참을 걸어도 아이를

사또의 사건일지

찾을 수 없었다. 이대로 놓치는 걸까. 돌아가서 이 씨라는 자를 추궁해야 하나. 점점 걸음이 느려졌다. 하지만 아이가 산으로 들어간 이상 두고 나갈 수는 없어 다리를 움직였다. 그때 저만치 앞 나무들 너머에서 환한 볕이 들어오는 게 보였다. 설마 벌써 그 커다란 산을 넘었단 말인가. 그때 아침에 들었던 명랑한 목소리가 빽빽한 나무를 뚫고 들려왔다.

"오라버니! 이제 다들 절대 나비를 못 찾을 거야. 그렇지?"
"아니야. 계속 주위를 살펴야 해. 이 나비처럼 오늘도 나비들이 새로 날아다닐 거야."
"정말? 그럼 언제까지 나비를 잡아야 해?"
"그건 알 수 없어. 하지만 우리가 이렇게 노력을 해야…"
오누이로 보이는 남매가 나무에 기대 볕을 쬐고 있었다. 성큼성큼 등 뒤로 다가갔다. "네 이놈들, 이런 위험한 산에 대체 왜…"

나무 그늘을 벗어나자 눈이 멀어버릴 것만 같은 강한 햇살이 온몸으로 쏟아져 내렸다. 동굴같이 어둡던 산에 익숙해져 있던 눈이 빛에 적응하지 못했다. 눈을 질끈 감았다가 천천히 떴다.

"… 이럴 수가."
잔뜩 겁을 집어먹은 오누이 뒤로 끝도 없이 펼쳐진 유채꽃이 나를 반겼다. 살면서 한 번도 본 적 없는 풍경이었다. 산 중턱이라고는 믿기지 않을 정도로 너른 유채꽃 밭이

박권

 바람에 따라 파도 치듯 쏴아아 흘러내렸다. 마치 햇살을 받아 반짝거리는 노란 비단을 펼쳐 놓은 것만 같았다. 그 사이사이 그렇게 애타게 찾던 나비들이 낮에 뜬 별처럼 파란 하늘을 가득 메우고 있었다. 천당에 간다면 이런 풍경을 볼 수 있을까. 나도 모르게 벌어진 턱을 다물 수 없었다. 저마다 다른 무늬를 가져 알록달록한 수십, 수백의 나비들이 멀쩡히 날아다니는 걸 보자 어제오늘 꽉 막혔던 가슴이 탁 트이는 기분이 들었다. 찾았다. 여기 있었구나. 전부 여기 있었어.
 "나으리, 죽을죄를 지었습니다."
 "살려 주세요⋯."
 오라비로 보이는 아이가 발치에 엎으려 고개를 숙이자 누이가 따라 얼굴을 묻고 울음을 터트렸다. 이를 어쩐다. 우선 나비를 찾은 데다 이런 위험한 산속에 아이들을 더 둘 수가 없어 손을 내밀었다.
 "일어나거라. 이 일은 관아에 가서 물을 테니 우선 내려가자꾸나."

 이른 시간부터 관아에 사람들이 몰렸다. 너른 마당에 덩그러니 서게 된 아이들이 안쓰러웠지만 잘잘못을 따져야 했다. 누이는 이미 지저분한 치마를 꽉 쥐어 잡고 닭똥 같은 눈물을 소리 없이 뚝뚝 흘리고 있었다. 얼른 끝내야 아이들이

사또의 사건일지

서둘러 집으로 돌아갈 수 있을 테니 자리에 앉아 이방에게 손짓을 했다.

"네가 나비를 전부 잡아들인 것이 맞느냐."

"… 예."

이방의 질문에 오라비라고 해봤자 막 열 살쯤 되어 보이는 사내아이가 고개를 끄덕였다. "마을 아이들이 부르는 노래를 퍼트린 것도 네가 맞느냐."

내가 묻자 아이가 대답 없이 고개를 끄덕였다. 나이에 어울리지 않게 결연한 얼굴이다.

"어찌 그랬느냐."

한참을 시위라도 하듯 입을 꾹 다물고 있던 아이가 숨을 크게 들이쉬고 말문을 열었다. "나비가 사라졌다고 동네 사람들에게 알려주기 위해 그리했습니다."

"나비가 사라진 걸 사람들이 알아야 했느냐."

"예."

"어째서?"

"… 그래야 나비를 잡지 못하니까요."

어째 이야기가 제자리를 빙빙 돌 낌새가 보였다. 훈장이 노래에 대한 이야기를 물어도 대답하지 않았다던 마을 아이들처럼 나비를 잡아다 빼돌린 이유를 쉽게 이야기하고 싶지 않은 모양이었다. 말이 길어지겠군. 이미 마을 사람들이 다 아는 사건이니 없던 일로 할 수도 없건만. 그때 관아 대문

박권

쪽에서 웅성거림이 들리더니 인파를 뚫고 다 헤진 옷차림의 부부가 뛰어 들어 왔다. 황망한 눈으로 마당을 두리번거리던 둘은 아이들을 끌어안아 이리저리 살피더니 흙바닥에 쏟아지듯 꿇어앉아 다 쉰 목소리로 살려 달라 빌기 시작했다.

"나으리. 뭣도 모르는 어린 것들이 한 일입니다. 제발 살려주십시오."

"벌이라면 아비인 제가 달게 받겠습니다. 제발 아이들을 풀어주시옵소서."

꿇어앉아 양손을 싹싹 비비는 부모님의 모습을 본 계집아이가 결국 큰 소리로 울음을 터뜨렸다. 이 재판 아닌 재판을 구경하던 사람들 사이에서 안타까운 탄식이 흘러나왔다. 이럴 생각은 전혀 없었는데. 꼭 나쁜 사람이 된 것 같아 당황스러워 엉거주춤 자리에서 일어났다.

"이보시게들, 진정하게나. 응? 우리 사또께서는 그리 야박하신 분이 아니야. 알지 않는가들."

내 표정을 본 이방이 두 부부에게로 다가가 팔을 잡고 일으켜 세웠다. 어머니 치맛자락을 꽉 붙든 딸아이의 등을 토닥이면서 이쪽을 올려다보는 시선들은 오래 굶기라도 한 듯 퀭했다.

"단지 아이가 왜 나비를 숨겼는지 이유를 알고 싶은 것뿐이네. 자네 부부도 알고 있었는가."

사또의 사건일지

　내 물음에 부부가 고개를 절레절레 저었다. 표정에 거짓은 전혀 묻어나지 않았다. "모릅니다요. 나비가 사라졌다는 건 소문을 들어 알았지만 저희 아이가 그랬다고는 상상조차 해본 적이 없습니다."
　다시 아이를 바라보았다. 꾹 다문 입술에 낭패감이 스치는 듯했다. 저 조그마한 게 대체 무슨 생각일까.
　"나비를 왜 숨겼느냐."
　관아에 몰려든 사람들이 숨죽이고 아이의 입에서 나올 말을 기다렸다. 그때 어머니의 다리에 찰싹 달라붙어 있던 누이가 울음을 그치고 야무지게 눈물을 훔치더니 쨍한 목소리로 말했다. "어머니 아버지가 헤어질지도 몰라서요!"
　나를 비롯한 이방, 마을 사람들, 아이의 부모까지 전부 지금 들은 말을 이해하지 못했다는 얼굴을 하고 아이들을 바라볼 수밖에 없었다. 나비를 숨긴 이유가 부모의 헤어짐을 막기 위해서라니. 그 둘이 어떤 연관이 있단 말인가. 누이의 발언에 오라비가 이제 다 끝났다는 듯 눈을 질끈 감았다. 마을 사람들이 저마다 계집아이 말의 속뜻을 유추하기 위해 수런거렸다.
　"며칠 전 밤, 부모님이 나누는 말씀을 들었습니다. 이대로라면 굶어 죽지 않기 위해서라도 나비를 주고받아야 한다고요."

박권

 사내아이가 드디어 입을 열었다. 모두 숨을 죽이고 아이의 말에 귀를 기울였다.
 "처음에는 무슨 뜻인지 몰랐습니다. 하지만 두 분의 이야기를 마저 들어보니 나비를 주고받는다는 것이 이제 우리 가족은 함께하지 못한다는 뜻이라는 걸 알게 되었습니다."
 그랬구나. 나도 모르게 참고 있던 숨이 탁 터져 나왔다. 마을 사람들 사이에서도 다시금 탄식만 쏟아졌을 뿐 관아가 조용해졌다. 그 나비가 살아 있는 나비일 거라 생각했다니. 혼인을 파할 때 주고받는 징표가 나비 모양과 닮아 나비를 주고받는다 말하는 것이거늘.
 "저희 부모님은 금실이 좋습니다. 땅 하나 없는 형편이지만 서로를 존중하고 저희를 아껴주십니다. 사이좋은 부모님이 가난 때문에 헤어지시는 걸 자식 된 도리로 막아야겠다 생각했습니다. 나비를 숨기고 제가 하루바삐 자라 두 분께서 부부의 연을 맺는 순간 약속한 백년해로를 지켜드리고 싶었습니다."
 눈물이 나올 것 같은지 아이가 두 주먹을 꽉 쥐었다. 아이 어머니는 소리 없이 눈물을 흘리기 시작했고 아비는 아이를 바라보며 말로써 설명할 수 없는 표정을 짓고 있었다.
 "그래서 나비를 숨겼습니다. 고을의 온 나비를 없애면 부모님이 나비를 주고받지 못하실 테니까요. 나비가 생각보다 많아 벗들의 도움을 받기도 했습니다. 허나 다 제가 부탁해서

사또의 사건일지

벌인 짓입니다. 벗들은 제 부탁 하나에 나비를 잡느라 고생한 잘못밖에 없습니다."

혹 도움을 준 벗들에게 해가 갈까 급하게 덧붙인다. 나이에 맞지 않게 철이 일찍 든 모양이다.

"… 노래를 퍼트린 건 잡을 수 있는 나비가 없다는 걸 부모님께 알려드려야 했기 때문입니다. 실은 어제 훈장님의 가르침으로 나비가 중요한 곤충이라는 걸 알았습니다. 허나 그만둘 수 없었습니다. 맹세코 나비를 죽이지 않았습니다. 나으리께서 보신 꽃밭에 전부 풀어주었습니다. 울창한 나무를 뚫고 다시 고을까지 날아오기 힘들 거라 생각해 먹이가 있는 꽃밭 쪽에 풀어준 것입니다. 제가 죽을죄를 지었습니다."

터지기 시작한 말은 막힌 물이 쏟아져 나오듯 막을 수 없어 보였다. 뺨이 발갛게 상기될 정도로 열을 올려 이야기한 아이가 마지막에 자그맣게 덧붙이며 주먹을 풀더니 고개를 숙였다.

"너희 부모가 주고받고자 했던 나비는 살아 있는 나비가 아닌 천으로 만든 나비다."

내 말에 아이가 고개를 번쩍 들었다. 당혹스러움에 크게 뜨인 눈이 나를 빤히 바라봤다.

"혼인을 파했다는 징표로 갖는 것이지. 그 나비를 살아 있는 나비라고 착각해 벌인 일이라는 건 알겠지만 고을의 나비를 전부 빼돌린 걸 그냥 넘어갈 수는 없다."

박권

　내내 어른스럽던 아이의 눈에 눈물이 차 반짝이는 게 보였다. 서둘러 판결을 내려야겠군.
　"허나 나비를 빼돌렸지만 죽게 두지 않고 안전한 곳에 풀어준 점을 감안해 다른 벌 대신 나비를 다시 고을에 돌려놓을 것을 명한다."
　이번에는 놀라움으로 아이의 눈이 더 크게 뜨였다. 저 어린것은 잘못이 없다.
　"동시에 내 살면서 한 번도 너처럼 효심이 깊은 자는 보지 못했다. 아직 어리지만 자식으로서 부모와 가족을 지키고자 하는 예를 높이 사 너희 부모가 나비를 주고받지 않도록 도와줄 것이다."
　아직 말뜻을 이해하지 못했는지 멍하니 서 있는 아이를 아비가 와락 끌어안았다. 그제야 눈을 깜빡이던 아이가 그 품에 안겨 울음을 터뜨렸다. 처음 만난 순간부터 지금까지 어른스레 굴었지만 부모 곁에서는 아직 어린아이일 뿐이었다. 주변에서 숨죽이며 지켜보던 마을 사람들이 서로 부둥켜안은 가족의 곁으로 와 축하의 말을 건넸다. 어쩐지 코끝이 시큰했다. 아래 서 있는 이방에게로 힐끔 시선을 돌리자 이미 옷소매로 눈물을 찍어 내느라 정신이 없어 보였다.

사또의 사건일지

[그리하여 고을 아이들과 함께 유채꽃이 가득한 산 중턱 공터에서 나비들을 조심스레 잡아 다시 마을 이곳저곳에 풀어주었습니다. 나비를 숨겼던 아이에게는 당장 필요한 쌀과 돈을, 그 부모에게는 효자를 길러낸 공을 치하해 자그마한 밭을 내렸습니다. 이제 가난으로 그 가족이 헤어지는 일을 일어나지 않겠지요. 전하, 예로부터 될성부른 나무는 떡잎부터 알아본다 합니다. 제 부모에게 이리 효심이 깊은 아이는 본 적이 없사옵니다. 훌륭하게 자라 전하의 곁에서 충신이 될 수도 있는 아이입니다. 부디 이 될성부른 떡잎에게 더 큰 세상으로 나아갈 수 있는 발판을 마련해주시길 청하옵니다.]

"하하하. 강원도로 간 박 당하관에게서 온 것이라 했지?"

"예. 그렇습니다, 전하."

"이것 참 재미있고 기특한 일이군. 글을 써 올린 당하관과 이 아이를 조정으로 부르도록 하거라. 내 직접 만나보고 싶구나."

"그리 하겠나이다."

물러나는 내시를 보던 왕이 다시 시선을 아래로 내렸다. 긴 내용을 읽으며 말아 두었던 두루마리 첫 부분을 펼치더니 다시금 찬찬히 읽어 내려가는 얼굴에 환한 미소가 슬그머니 떠올랐다.

사또의 사건일지
ⓒ 나비와북, 2024. Printed in Korea

지은이	박권
번역	유경하
표지 디자인	Joe Fitz
내지 편집	Joe Fitz
전화	010-8227-8359
홈페이지	nabiwabook.com
이메일	nabiwabook2021@naver.com
블로그	blog.naver.com/nabiwabook2021
인스타그램	instagram.com/nabiwabook_publisher
출판일	2024년 12월 20일
ISBN	979-11-989928-0-2
값	6,000 원
일러스트 저작권	ⓒ 2024

- 이 책의 판권은 지은이와 나비와북(Nabiwabook)에 있습니다.
- 이 책에 실린 내용의 무단 전제와 무단 복제를 금합니다.
- 이 책 내용의 전부 또는 일부를 재사용하려면 반드시 양측의 서면 동의를 받아야 합니다.